TALES FROM THE CRYPT

VOLUME 4

Introduced by the Crypt-Keeper

Story adaptations by Eleanor Fremont

Random House 🏠 New York

The stories in this volume first appeared in different form in *Tales from
the Crypt Comic Books* and *Shock SuspenStories Comic Books*
in the following years:

Tales from the Crypt

"The Substitute." Copyright © 1954 by I. C. Publishing Co., Inc.
Copyright renewed 1982 by William M. Gaines, Agent.

"Oil's Well That Ends Well." Copyright © 1952 by I. C. Publishing Co., Inc.
Copyright renewed 1980 by William M. Gaines, Agent.

"Death's Turn." Copyright © 1950 by I. C. Publishing Co., Inc.
Copyright renewed 1978 by William M. Gaines, Agent.

"The Craving Grave." Copyright © 1953 by I. C. Publishing Co., Inc.
Copyright renewed 1981 by William M. Gaines, Agent.

Shock SuspenStories

"The Big Stand-up." Copyright © 1952 by Tiny Tot Comics, Inc.
Copyright renewed 1980 by William M. Gaines, Agent.

"Raw Deal." Copyright © 1954 by Tiny Tot Comics, Inc.
Copyright renewed 1982 by William M. Gaines, Agent.

Library of Congress Cataloging-in-Publication Data
Fremont, Eleanor. Tales from the crypt.
    Adaptations of: Tales from the crypt / William M. Gaines.
    Vol. 1 introduced by the Crypt-Keeper; v. 2 introduced by the Old Witch;
v. 3 introduced by the Vault-Keeper; v. 4 introduced by the Crypt-Keeper;
v. 5 introduced by the Old Witch.
    Vol. 3 adapted by Richard Wenk.
    A collection of horror stories, featuring such grisly characters as a
vampire, werewolf, and murderous madman.
    1. Horror tales, American.   2. Children's stories, American.
3. Horror stories.   4. Short stories.
I. Wenk, Richard. II. Gaines, William M. Tales from the crypt.
PZ7.F8867 Tal 1991 [Fic] 90-23916 ISBN 0-679-81799-9 (v. 1 : pbk.)
ISBN 0-679-81800-6 (v. 2 : pbk.) ISBN 0-679-81801-4 (v. 3 : pbk.)
ISBN 0-679-83073-1 (v. 4 : pbk.) ISBN 0-679-83074-X (v. 5 : pbk.)

Manufactured in the United States of America 10 9 8 7 6 5 4 3 2 1

CONTENTS

FROM THE
CRYPT-KEEPER

 *Hello, hello, hello again, my delicious little droolings—er, darlings. So nice to see you once more! Have you been getting your minimum daily requirement of slime? Good, good, good. And I hope you haven't been forgetting to brush your fangs. Nobody likes yellow fangs.*

I myself have been keeping very busy. So little time, so much to do. There are the rats and spiders to feed, of course, and the crypt door is just impossible to keep creaky.

Well, I guess you've just been panting for some more stories from the depths. You'll be glad to hear that I haven't been shirking. I've been scouring the dankest corners of the earth for you, my petite plump ones. Just wait till you see what I've found.

The first one, called "The Substitute," has a bit

of a French flair. It's about a fellow named Henri Duval, who learns a lesson: Careful planning is important. You can learn a lot from this story. In fact, now that I think of it, all these stories are just chock-full of Life's Little Lessons.

Take the second story, for example: "Oil's Well That Ends Well." Phil and Sam learn something about nasty habits in this one. I'll say no more.

The third story, "Death's Turn," offers a moral that's a helpful one for you and me: It's not nice to kill people. Keep that in mind, won't you?

Number four is called "The Big Stand-up," and it has something really <u>big</u> to teach us. Maybe I'll just let you figure out what it is. There'll be a test on it tomorrow.

Story number five, "The Craving Grave," teaches us that you can't be too careful about people's feelings. And not just people's feelings, either. It appears that graves have feelings too. I never knew that, did you? I mean, where will it all end? Saltshakers? Doorknobs? Give me a break here.

And lastly, but not leastly, there's a really delectable little morsel called "Raw Deal." I know you'll love it to bits. Why? Because you're <u>you</u>.

Oozily yours,
The Crypt-Keeper

Slog right up, my little dears, for the first story in my tasty smorgasbord. To get into the right frame of mind for it, you have to imagine the equatorial jungle. Giant leeches. Spiders as big as your hand. Snakes as thick as your leg. Great green gobs of—well, you get the picture. Ready? Here we go!

THE SUBSTITUTE

For seven long years, Henri Duval had suffered the equatorial heat and the blazing sun and the tortured labors of the French penal colony — all because he'd poisoned the husband of the woman he'd loved. For seven long years, he'd sweated and slaved, hacking clearings into that jungle island from which there was no escape. It was an impossible task, for no sooner had a tract been cleared than the relentless tropical overgrowth closed in again like a green tide. But this was the punishment for murder, and Henri was forced to undergo its rigors, left only to dream of cool Paris and cool wine and the cool lips of a woman. And then, one day, he discovered the herb, really just an unassuming little plant on the floor of the jungle.

"*Sacré Dieu!*" he said to himself. "Good Lord! It's hellebore!"

Henri was an expert on poisons, and he knew hellebore: the herb with the rootstock that yielded the poisonous glucoside called helleborin. He immediately tore the plant from the spongy jungle floor, stuffing the short roots into the shirt of his prison uniform.

"Hey, you!" shouted the prison guard, fingering the trigger of his rifle. "Duval! Keep that

machete going! Or else the governor will have you flogged to within an inch of your life!" Henri knew this was not an empty threat. The governor, hated by everyone on the island, would not hesitate to have a prisoner whipped for looking at him the wrong way.

By the time the blazing equatorial sun had sunk into the western sky and the exhausted, bedraggled prisoners been marched back into the penal colony compound, Henri Duval had made his plans.

"They brag that no one has ever escaped from this island purgatory," he muttered fiercely to himself. "Well, I . . . Henri Duval . . . will be the first!"

That night, Henri hid the hellebore roots in his mattress, and the next day he began to gather the things he needed. When the clearing crews were again marched out into the steaming jungle, he chose just the right size of bamboo stalk, hacking it off with his machete. Farther on, he carefully gathered just the right shape of palm fronds. And then, when the guard wasn't looking, he hacked off the perfect amount of cork bark from a tree.

These he hid in his shirt, and that evening

he successfully smuggled them into the compound. Late that night, when the other prisoners were asleep, Henri worked. With the knife he'd stolen from the mess hall, he carefully carved the chunk of cork bark into a smooth, round teardrop shape, which barely fit into the palm of his hand.

Slitting the elongated end of his cork teardrop, he inserted the correctly shaped palm fronds, trimming them down until they fit. He now had a basic missile, whose flight would be steadied by the palm fronds, much the way feathers steady the flight of an arrow.

Next, into the bulbous end of the cork teardrop, he inserted the needle he'd taken from a fellow prisoner's sewing kit and . . . *voilà!* Henri had fashioned an accurate dart, a dart that would be poisoned—and then blown through the hollow bamboo stalk he'd cut in the jungle.

All that night, Henri practiced with his blowgun until his aim was deadly. The only sound that could be heard was the soft *thunk* of the dart hitting his homemade target.

Finally, he hid his murderous weapon,

along with the hellebore roots, in his mattress, and lay down for the few hours of sleep left to him. "If all goes well," he thought to himself, "I, Henri Duval, will be in Paris next month!"

The next day, Henri found two flat rocks and smuggled them back into the compound, as he had done with the other things. That night, he used them to grind down the hellebore roots, carefully catching the juice that ran from the pulverized meat in a tin cup. Then he dipped his dart-needle into the highly toxic poison. Then he went to bed and slept a sleep made sweet with dreams of French food and French ladies.

And the next morning, as the loathed governor of the penal colony strode across the compound's grounds on his daily constitutional, Henri stood at his window, took careful aim, and let fly his lethal missile.

"*Mon Dieu!*" cried the governor as the needle pierced his back. "My God!"

By nightfall, the governor was dead.

A poor unfortunate prisoner, in whose mattress the blowgun had been found, was

whipped to death, vainly protesting his innocence to the last.

And since Henri was thought to be a good worker, he was assigned, with two other prisoners, the job of building the governor's coffin. It was in this coffin that the governor's body would be kept until the arrival of the monthly ship from the Continent.

Henri had planned it all. The governor had been a famous French naval hero, and Henri had known that his body would be shipped back to France. He'd counted on it. This was Henri Duval's plot, the means for his escape.

Henri and the other two worked on the coffin late into the night, hammering and sawing in silence. But when Henri began drilling holes in the side of the coffin, one of his compatriots looked at him strangely. *"Air holes?"* said the man incredulously. "Why, Henri? The cursed *chien*, the dog, is dead. Why does he need air holes for his coffin?"

Henri just smiled. "To allow for expanding gases, *mon ami*," he explained.

No one said anything further, and they kept working.

The night before the monthly steamer's expected arrival, Henri slipped from his barracks and hurried to the chapel, where the governor's body lay in state in the crude coffin. Nobody was around.

Quickly, Henri stripped the body of its clothes and dressed it in his grimy prison uniform.

Then he slashed and hacked the face until it was unrecognizable. Henri carried the disfigured corpse into the barracks and placed it quietly on his cot. In the morning, he knew, they would find the body and think that an enemy of Henri Duval's had attacked and murdered him during the night.

Then he took the food he'd hoarded and the can of rainwater he'd collected and hurried back across the compound to the chapel. There, he climbed into the recently vacated coffin to wait . . . to wait for them to come and carry him to the boat and eventual freedom. Having to lie in a dark, cramped coffin was a small price to pay for the new life he was soon to begin.

The next morning, footsteps approached. Suddenly, Henri heard pounding and hammering above him.

"*Sacré Dieu!*" he screamed silently. "They are nailing me—Henri Duval—in!"

At first, Henri was terrified. But then he calmed down as he realized that he would only have to effect a small change of plans.

"*Rien,*" he said to himself, thinking it through. "It's nothing. When I get to France, I will certainly have an opportunity to free myself."

Henri was overjoyed as he felt his coffin lifted by many arms and carried out of the chapel, across the compound, down to the penal colony's wharf, and up the gangplank of the supply ship.

He listened with glee to the shriek of the liner's whistle, the muffled roar of its engines. He felt the gentle heaving as the ship backed off from the pier and headed into the open sea. Away! Away from that cursed place at last!

As Henri settled in for the long journey, he began to think ahead. He had been so busy planning the murder of the governor, he had devoted little thought to his long trip in the dark coffin. Now he calculated the approximate length of the voyage and realized that he would have to put himself on a strict rationing program in order to make his meager food supply last. It was hours later when he afforded himself his first morsel of food, washed down by one gulp of the tepid water.

That night, the humming of the ship's engines lulled Henri into a peaceful sleep in the dark and quiet of his coffin bed.

But the next morning, he was awakened rudely as the coffin was lifted brusquely and carried out onto the deck.

Henri's eyes looked wildly around his little coffin. "What now?" he wondered, trying not to panic.

He listened as the engines stopped and only the gentle lapping of the ocean waves drifted through the coffin's air holes. And then he heard the captain's voice, droning on about something. . . .

". . . and so, in compliance with Governor Milleux's last request," the captain was saying. . . .

Henri's blood froze in his veins as he felt the coffin being lifted to the ship's rail and sliding forward, pointing toward the water.

". . . we commit the coffin containing his

body to the deep, for burial at sea. . . ."

Henri's scream was cut short as the coffin hit the tossing brine. Saltwater poured in through the air holes, filling his pine prison, filling his blubbering mouth, filling his gasping lungs.

"*Yaaaaaa!*" he shrieked. "I, Henri Duval, am drowning!" But nobody heard him screaming, and nobody heard the quiet gurgle the

scream became, as the governor's coffin began its dignified, stately descent to the bottom of the sea.

Well, my little darlings, I've got a sinking feeling that happy Henri's story is just about over. Ocean travelers in that part of the world, I'm told, will sometimes hear a ghastly voice singing a little song that's carried along by the ocean breezes. It ends, ". . . and all that he could see, see, see was the bottom of the deep blue sea, sea, sea. . . ."

 *Listen closely, kiddies, because you can learn a lot from the title of this story. It's a very old saying. It puts me in mind of some other old sayings too—like "The oily boid catches the woim." Or "Oily to bed, oily to rise, something, something, I forget." Anyhow, I'll stop gushing now, because—*

OIL'S WELL
THAT ENDS WELL

The flashy convertible came to a stop at a point on the highway overlooking the sprawling Midwestern town. The two men looked down at the rooftops and smiled.

"Well, Phil," said the man who was driving, "there she is, waiting for us. Like a sitting duck waiting to be plucked."

The other man took a deep drag on his cigarette and squinted down at the town below. "There's the park," he said. "Down there in the center of town. And there's the cemetery, over there."

19

The driver turned to the man with the cigarette between his lips. "Phil!" he said. "How many times have I told you not to talk with that butt hanging out of your mouth? It doesn't look good."

"Huh?" said Phil. "Oh. I'm sorry, Sam. I forgot." He took the cigarette out of his mouth, knocking ashes all over his lap.

"Well, don't forget!" Sam was annoyed. "After all, you're supposed to be an honest businessman! You look like a sharpie when you do that."

"Okay, okay! Don't get excited, Sam. I'll be careful." Phil put the cigarette out in the ashtray, just to show what a careful guy he was.

The car continued down the highway and then into town. It pulled up in front of the only hotel.

"All right," said Sam quietly. "On your toes, Phil. Here we go. I'll start getting the suitcases out. You check in."

"Right, Sam."

Sam started to unload the luggage from the flashy convertible while Phil entered the hotel and crossed the lobby to the desk. The hotel had been a good one, perhaps fifty years ago. The flowered carpeting was a little threadbare now, and the heavy velvet curtains were just a bit tattered at the bottom.

"Howdy, stranger," said the balding, bow-tied desk clerk. "What can I do for yuh?"

Phil tapped the ashes from his cigarette into the man's inkwell. "I'd like two rooms," he said. "One for myself and one for my field man."

"Field man?" inquired the desk clerk. "What's that?"

"Allow me to introduce myself," said Phil

with a certain modesty. "My name is Philip Garson. Oil's my business. I locate oil deposits for big oil companies. My field man, Mr. Simpson, handles the general surveying of prospective sites. We're just passing through."

"Oil, eh?" said the desk clerk, scratching his chin. He pushed the hotel register toward Phil. "Sign here," he said.

Phil signed the register in a sweeping hand, sprinkling ashes all over the leather-bound book.

"Thinking of looking around these parts?" asked the desk clerk casually.

"Thank you. Er—no," said Phil. "We're on our way north."

Sam came into the lobby, loaded down with the suitcases. "Where should I put the luggage, Mr. Garson?" he asked.

The desk clerk pointed toward the wide, curving stairway. "Rooms 201 and 202," he said. "Up them stairs and to the right."

"You heard the gentleman, Simpson," said Phil, blowing a thin stream of smoke out his nose.

"Yes sir," said Sam. He shot Phil a nasty look over his shoulder as he climbed the stairs.

The man behind the desk watched as Sam carried the luggage up the stairs, and Phil followed. Then he bent toward a man who had been sitting on the lobby settee, reading the newspaper.

"Psst! Hey, Jess!" he whispered. "Didja hear that? The dapper lookin' guy's an oil man!"

Jess, who spent most of his free time (which was *all* his time) sitting in the hotel lobby, put down his paper. He hadn't really been reading it anyhow. "He must be rich," said Jess. "Take a gander at the car parked outside."

The two of them peered out the glass doors at the fancy red car.

Meanwhile, upstairs, out of earshot, Sam was whispering angrily to Phil. "What's the big idea, talking to that clerk with that cigarette dangling from your mouth? What are you trying to do, queer the deal?"

"Huh?" said Phil, looking around. "Oh, the cigarette." He took it out of his mouth and ground it out in the bathroom sink. "I—I forgot, Sam. I'm sorry."

"I'll give you such a hit," said Sam.

Later, as night came on, a group of people

from the town gathered in the hotel lobby, as they often did. Phil was there too, chatting in a neighborly way. He'd been talking about the oil business.

"A hundred thousand dollars, Mr. Garson?" said Jess disbelievingly to Phil. "That's a lot of money."

"That's what the Bayshore Oil Company paid," said Phil cheerfully, waving his cigarette for emphasis. "My commission was ten percent."

"And that's all you do? Locate oil deposits? And when the big oil companies buy, you collect your commission from the owner of the land?"

"Right," said Phil.

"Shucks," said another man. "Seems to me you'd be better off doin' the drillin' yourself."

"A lot better off," Phil agreed. "You're right. But drilling equipment costs a great deal, sir." He paused to brush a smoldering ash off his pants before it burned a hole. "It costs more money than I've got. I'd have to borrow—"

"Mr. Garson! Mr. Garson!" It was Sam, bursting through the front door.

"That's his field man, Mr. Simpson," explained the desk clerk to those assembled.

24

"Mr. Garson!" cried Sam, pulling Phil to one side. "I've got to speak to you—privately!"

"That's all right, Simpson," said Phil. "Out with it. You're all excited. What's up?"

The people in the lobby watched Sam with great interest.

"Oil, Mr. Garson!" cried Sam. "I'm sure of it!"

The room crupted.

"Oil?"

"Where?"

"Where is it?"

Phil took Sam by the sleeve. "Better come upstairs, Simpson!" he said.

Sam followed Phil up the stairs. Behind them, the hotel lobby buzzed with excitement.

"They found oil—" blurted one.

"—right here in town!" another finished.

"Anybody see where that Simpson feller come from?" asked Jess.

Upstairs in their room, the two men smiled. Phil opened the door a crack and peered out. He could just see the lobby.

"There's a crowd gathering, Sam," he chuckled. "Did you take care of it?"

"Nobody was around," replied Sam smugly. "I took care of it, all right. She'll ooze for a week! Now go ahead downstairs and start the pitch—but douse that cigarette first, will you, please?"

"Huh?" said Phil. "Oh, right." He put the cigarette out in a coffee cup.

Five minutes later, Phil came downstairs. The lobby of the hotel was jammed with townsfolk. Word traveled fast in a place like this.

Phil stopped halfway down the staircase and surveyed the crowd. "I'd like to see the mayor," he said.

"I'm the mayor," said a man toward the rear. "Jordon's my name."

"Mayor Jordon," said Phil, putting a friendly arm around the man, "I have been advised by my field man that there is oil on the town's property—under the city park."

"The park!" gasped the mayor.

"Hey!" yelled a man to the crowd. "There's oil under the park!"

"The town is rich!" cried somebody.

"Shall we go on over, Mayor Jordon?" asked Phil, smiling.

"Let's go, Mr. Garson!" replied the mayor.

In short order, the crowd stood around the black slick that seeped from the ground in the park. Everyone was trying to get a feel of the wonderful, gooey, smelly stuff.

"There are two things you can do, Mayor Jordon," Phil advised him. "You can turn the land over to a private oil company or drill for it yourselves."

"But *we* don't know anything about drilling for oil!" exclaimed the mayor.

Phil rubbed his chin and blew out a big puff of smoke. The mayor coughed.

"Well—I could handle it for you," mused Phil, "but it would cost a great deal. About a hundred and sixty thousand dollars."

"A hundred and sixty thousand dollars!" gasped the mayor. "But we couldn't afford—"

"Say, Mayor," interrupted someone in the crowd. "Why couldn't you let us folks in town put up the money? Form a corporation and issue stock!"

Mayor Jordon turned to the crowd. "What do you say, folks?" he asked them. "Do we turn the land over to a private company, or raise the money and drill for the oil ourselves?"

"Ourselves!" hollered several voices.

"Yeah! Let's keep it in the family!" someone added.

Phil stayed with the excited crowd for a while longer, and then went back to the hotel room, where Sam was waiting.

"They fell for it, Sam!" he said when the door was safely closed. "They're going to form a corporation and issue stock! And guess who they put in charge of drilling? *Me!*" He laughed so hard, he almost cried. "Where's my matches?" he said, patting down his pockets.

"I don't know," said Sam. "You shouldn't

smoke so much. Okay, now, as soon as they turn the money over to us, we'll pull the routine. . . ."

In the following days, a corporation was formed. Stock was issued, and subscriptions from the hardworking townsfolk poured in. They lined up outside Mayor Jordon's office to get their part of the oil well that was going to make them all rich.

"Here's a thousand dollars, Mayor Jordon," said Mr. Fagin. "That's all we could scrape up."

"That's fine, Mr. Fagin," said the mayor as he wrote a receipt. "Here's your ten shares."

Finally, everything was ready. Phil sat across from the mayor at a table in the hotel lobby, and the mayor pushed an envelope toward him. "Well, Mr. Garson," said the mayor, "the stock issue has been sold . . . every last share. Here's your check for a hundred and sixty thousand dollars. Oops, don't let that burning ash fall on it."

"Huh?" said Phil. "Oh, sorry. Anyway, this is very good. Now we can start the drilling."

In half an hour, Phil sat in the hotel room, watching Sam play solitaire on his suitcase. Sam cheated. Phil knew it.

"Here's the dough, Sam," said Phil. "I just cashed the check. Why don't we just skip town and forget the cemetery routine this time?"

"No!" barked Sam. "We'll want to work this deal again. You've got to be kept in the clear. The cemetery routine stays!"

Sam put down the last king and picked up the cards. "And just to make sure you don't forget to come and dig me up," he said, "*I'll* hide the dough. Now give me one of those pills and phone the mayor. You know what to say."

"Here y'are," said Phil, handing Sam a small bottle of black pills and reaching for the phone.

"S'long," said Sam. He opened the door and then paused. "Don't forget," he said. "Dig me up within six hours after they bury me. We'll pick up the dough on the way out of town. And for cryin' out loud, Phil, would you ditch that cigarette?"

"Huh?" said Phil. "Oh, I forgot. S'long, Sam." Sam closed the door behind him.

Mayor Jordon rushed to Philip Garson's hotel room in answer to Phil's frantic phone call.

"What do you mean, the oil deposit's phony?" he demanded.

"It's true," said Phil miserably. "When I found Simpson, my field man, gone, and the drilling money too, I checked. He poured oil into that sandy spot in the park! There's no oil there! We've been taken! Conned!"

"We'll get him," said a grim Mayor Jordon. "He won't get far."

Just outside of town, they did indeed find the flashy convertible, its front end rammed into a tree. Soon, a crowd had gathered to look.

"He's dead," said one of the town's two po-
licemen. "Heart attack, probably."

"Did you find the money?" someone asked
the mayor.

"Nope, not a dollar," sighed the mayor.

Phil Garson was taken to the police station
and questioned carefully. He broke down in
tears.

"I . . . I trusted him!" he sobbed. "He'd
been with me almost a year! I can't believe it!
First, lying about the oil . . . then stealing the
money . . . and now this! Dead! I'm—I'm so
sorry for all the folks that trusted me!" He buried his face in his hands.

"It wasn't your fault," said the patrolman.
"Do you have any idea what he might have
done with the money, Mr. Garson?"

Phil looked up in shock and amazement.
"Didn't he have it with him?" he said.

"No," said the patrolman. "We searched
carefully. His clothes, the car. He probably hid
it somewhere planning to come back and get it.
Now it's lost—for good."

A little later, after Phil had managed to
overcome his grief a bit, he showed up at the
town morgue. "I'd like to claim the body," he

said. "You know, give him a decent burial."

"Of course, Mr. Garson," said the man. "I'll give you a release."

And so, that afternoon, Sam Simpson was buried. Only the mayor, the gravedigger, the undertaker, and Phil were present to mourn the passing of the miserable crook. Naturally, Phil had made sure that Sam's "body" was not embalmed.

And several hours later, when the effects of the pill Sam had taken wore off, he woke up six feet under the earth. He wasn't scared; he was used to it.

This time, though, something was different. "Hey," he said to himself. "What's *that?* Something sticky—oozing into the coffin! Muddy water. Smells funny . . ."

The warm, thick liquid continued to seep into the coffin as the hours dragged by. Sam was almost overcome by the stench of it.

"Phil will be here soon," he said aloud to comfort himself. "He'll dig me out. Phew! That smell!"

The awful ooze puddled higher and higher in the coffin. It rose above Sam's ears. Now he was really starting to get scared.

"Phil!" he cried. "Phil, for Pete's sake, hurry! Before I drown in here!" He thrashed about. What *was* that *smell?*

Sam was pressing his face against the satin lid of the coffin, sucking at the last traces of air, when the digging sounded from above.

"It's Phil!" Sam whooped. "Thank the Lord! Hurry, Phil! Boy, will I be glad to see your stupid face with that dangling cigarette . . . and . . . and . . . now I know what that stuff smells like! Oh, Lord!"

And as Phil lifted the lid of the coffin, Sam screamed at him, his black, shining face rising from the surface of the ooze-filled coffin. His eyes looked very white against the black, as they flashed insanely at Phil.

"It's oil . . . Phil!"

"Huh?" said Phil.

The cigarette dangling from Phil's mouth dropped into the thick black oil as his jaw fell open in astonishment. Suddenly, there was an enormous blinding white flash.

Phaaarooooomm!

Heh, heh, heh! Yep, Phil forgot again, and this time, Sam really blew up! Of course, so did Phil. In fact, he really went to pieces over his bad habit. But look at the bright side: The town got its oil boom after all.

Well, gotta go. Oil be seeing you—next story. Ta-ta!

This story brings another wonderful old saying to mind: "Life has its little ups and downs." Or maybe a better saying for this story is from the world of science: "What goes up must come down." Pay attention now, and you might learn something you can use in school. Then again, maybe not. . . .

DEATH'S TURN

A lone figure carrying a leather briefcase stands on the deserted midway of a run-down amusement park.

"Hmmm," the man says to himself, surveying the rotted floorboards, tattered canvas, and boarded-up concessions, "this place certainly is a flop. Not a customer around."

At that same moment, down at the other end of the empty midway in a shack marked OFFICE, two men are talking.

"We won't be able to keep open another week, Kane," says the pale man in the straw hat.

"There must be a way to get folks out here,

Crossen," says the other, a tall, gaunt fellow in a bowler. "We can't be licked yet!" He gazes thoughtfully into the blue cigar smoke. "We need something different," he muses. "Something that no amusement park around here has."

"A super attraction, eh, Kane?" says Crossen.

Suddenly there is a knock on the door, and the man carrying the briefcase enters the shack.

"Yeah, bud?" says Kane. "What can we do for you?" They are not used to receiving visitors.

"Are you the owners of this amusement park?" asks the stranger. He is a pleasant-looking gent, with thick glasses and a little pencil mustache.

"Yes," says Kane. "We're the unfortunate ones."

"Gentlemen," says the stranger with a winning smile, "your problems are solved."

Kane and Crossen look at each other. Probably just another kook.

"Allow me to introduce myself," says the man. "I am Robert Bixby, construction engineer." He holds up his briefcase. "Here in this briefcase I have plans for a new type of high-speed roller coaster!"

"But we have a roller coaster," objects Kane.

"That old thing!" scoffs Bixby. "It's outdated. I have designed a roller coaster far superior to those found in any amusement park in the world! It is faster, and it has sharper drops. One is almost straight down for *two hundred feet*—as high as a twenty-story building!"

"Kane!" shouts Crossen. "This is it! Just what we need!"

"Yes, Crossen," Kane agrees, completely won over. "I can see it now! 'The fastest roller coaster in the world!'. . .'We dare you to ride

it!'" He sweeps his hands through the air in excitement.

Crossen doesn't need to hear any more. "Mister, we'll buy it!" he says. "Let's see the plans!"

"Ah, gentlemen," says Bixby hesitatingly, "there's just one stipulation."

Kane's eyes narrow. "Strings attached?" he says.

"Okay," says Crossen. "What's your proposition?"

Bixby holds up the suitcase again and gives it a tantalizing little shake. "For these plans, I want to be taken in as a partner in the amusement park," he says.

The men are outraged. "A partner!" sputters Kane. "Why, that's highway robbery!"

"Take it or leave it," says Bixby, turning to leave. "There are other men who'd be willing to—"

"Okay, okay," says Kane. "It's a deal. We'll draw up the necessary papers."

"Good," says Bixby. "As soon as we're all signed up, I'll show you the plans—and a working model that I've constructed."

The next night, the three men meet at Robert Bixby's home. Documents are produced and spread out over the big desk. Hands are shaken.

"Now that the papers are all signed and in order, Bixby," says Crossen, "how about showing us this 'super roller coaster'?"

"All right, gentlemen," says Bixby. "This way."

Bixby leads Kane and Crossen into a large room and turns on the lights. "There it is, gentlemen," he says. "A scale model!"

The model is about four feet high, very detailed, full of amazing curves, climbs, and drops. But . . . something looks a little different about it.

"Looks kinda queer to me," says Kane, narrowing his eyes and rubbing his chin. He is squinting at the track. Instead of looking like a regular roller coaster track, the runway curves up at the sides.

Bixby smiles his mysterious little smile. "It's built on the principle of a bobsled," he explains. "No rails. The curved runway is scientifically banked at each turn and drop. This reduces friction and allows greater speed."

He points to the model. "The first drop," he says, "is practically straight down. A slight twist in the curved track keeps the car from actually becoming a free-falling body. The speed gathered here will be between one hundred and one hundred five miles per hour."

He continues walking around the model, pointing as he goes. "There follows a series of turns, banks, rises, and more drops calculated to maintain this speed throughout the ride. The car is stopped by a two-hundred-foot incline, which it climbs under its own power. It is then ready to begin again."

"Amazing! Absolutely amazing!" says Crossen.

"How soon can construction on this 'eighth wonder' begin?" asks Kane.

"Immediately," says Bixby.

"'Eighth wonder'!" exclaims Crossen, clapping Kane on the shoulder. "Say, that's great! That's what we'll call it! The 'Eighth Wonder of the World'!"

And so, work on the "new super roller coaster" is begun. Soon, giant fingers of steel point skyward.

The three partners take a walk around the bustling construction site.

"Bixby," says Kane, "your brainchild had

better be all you say it is—or else!"

"We've sunk every last cent we've got in this!" says Crossen.

"Don't worry, gentlemen," Bixby reassures them. "Mathematical figures cannot lie. It will work."

Little by little, as the days and weeks go by, the colossus takes shape. Girder is attached to girder, the specially made concave track is delivered, and the rocket-like cars are settled into its grooves.

Hands clasped behind their backs, the three men look up at the thing. "Well, gentlemen," says Bixby, "it is almost complete."

And then, the long-awaited day arrives when the last rivet is driven home, and the "Eighth Wonder of the World" is completed.

"Finished—at last!" crows Crossen triumphantly.

"How soon till we open for business?" Kane asks Bixby.

"Patience, gentlemen," says the engineer and third partner. "First there are some tests to be made."

"Tests?" says Kane. "We thought you had this all worked out."

"But you said—" says Crossen.

"*Mathematically* it should work perfectly," Bixby explains, squinting through his thick glasses. "But if there was any error in the construction—well, we must test it to find out."

And so, the next day, the sandbag test is made. Bixby hauls a large bag of sand out of his car and up to the roller coaster, and heaves it into the front seat of a shiny red rocket car.

"What's this sandbag test for, Bixby?" asks Kane rather testily.

"The sandbags represent our future riders," Bixby tells him. "This test will show us if a human being will remain in the car as it takes the turns and banks—or will be thrown from it."

The red car is moved to the top of the track and released. It rolls down an incline, gathering speed. Then it reaches the first drop. At a hundred and six miles per hour, it plummets earthward.

"Everything seems to be going according to calculations," says Bixby.

"Whew!" whistles Kane. "Look at that car go!"

"People will be coming from all over to ride this baby," says Crossen gleefully.

The test is a success. The sandbags remain in the car, which returns from its first ride completely unscathed.

That night, champagne is uncorked, glasses are clinked, and toasts are offered.

"Gentlemen," says Bixby, squinting at his partners through his glasses, "I drink to the success of our amusement park!" It takes him a couple of tries before his glass connects with those of the others.

"Success!" says Kane.

"Success!" echoes Crossen.

But later, after Bixby leaves, Crossen turns to Kane with a sour look on his face. "Did you hear him?" he says. "*Our* amusement park! He's a partner! But it was *our* money, Kane! Yours and mine!"

"Yeah," says Kane, "we were fools to give him a partnership."

"But there's a way of getting it back, Kane! A way of getting rid of him!"

"You mean . . . kill him?"

"Why not? We can make it look like an accident."

"What's your plan, Crossen?" asks Kane.

The next morning, Kane and Crossen meet Bixby at the park. The early sun sparkles on the brand-new roller coaster, and the sky is blue.

"What's up, Kane?" asks Bixby. "Why did you ask me here?"

"Crossen here noticed something funny as the car made the big drop yesterday," says Kane.

"Yes," adds Crossen. "Let's go over there."

He points to the roller coaster. "I'll show you as the car passes us. Kane, here, can start the car after we get there."

The two men make their way to the bottom of the two-hundred-foot drop. Then Crossen signals Kane to release the car.

"Now lean over and watch that spot there. Here she comes!" says Crossen as they lean way out over the track at its lowest point.

"After this," says Bixby, "there's one more test to make, Crossen. I—"

But he doesn't get to explain what the last test is supposed to be, for as the car, still loaded with sandbags, hurtles down the almost perpendicular incline, Crossen pushes Bixby right into its path.

Bixby's scream is almost drowned out by the rumble of the roller coaster rocket car. Almost, but not quite.

He is killed instantly. A ton of steel flying at a hundred and five miles per hour packs a mighty wallop.

They call it an unfortunate accident and keep it quiet. Kane and Crossen know that the publicity might harm business.

Very soon, opening day arrives, and the two

partners stand at the office window surveying the excited throngs.

"Well, today's the big day, Kane," says Crossen.

"Yeah, and look at 'em flocking in already!" says Kane with glee.

Yes, the crowds have come from all over, as Kane had predicted. They fill the newly renovated amusement park, each person clamoring to be the first to ride the "Eighth Wonder of the World."

Kane stands at a microphone before the crowd. "Ladies and gentlemen!" he proclaims.

"I think it is only fitting that before we open this wondrous roller coaster to you, the public, my partner and I, who built and planned it, ride it first!"

The two eager men get into the car and sit down.

"Imagine, Crossen," smirks Kane as they settle into their seats. "Poor Bixby never even got to ride his own brainchild!"

"Tch, tch," Crossen chuckles. "A shame, Kane. A crying shame!"

The car is released, and it begins to move down the incline, gathering speed.

"Here comes the first drop, Kane!" says Crossen, a bit apprehensively.

"I'm going to close my eyes!" quavers Kane. "I'm—afraid!"

The crowd is still. A hush has fallen over it. The only sound heard is the whirring of the roller coaster car over its curved track.

"Here they come!" cries someone in the crowd. "They're coming back!" The roller coaster has made its complete circuit.

The car moves up the two-hundred-foot incline and comes to a stop. But the two men inside it don't move. They just sit there, leering

. . . their heads at a grotesque angle . . . their eyes bulging . . .

"What the—" says somebody.

"They're dead! Both of them!"

"Their necks are broken!"

Of course, Kane and Crossen can't hear the hubbub. They just stare sightlessly at the Eighth Wonder of the World.

Hee, hee! That's right, they were dead! Their necks were snapped like dried twigs! Hee, hee! Yep, it <u>was</u> the fastest roller coaster in the world! So fast . . . that no human being could survive the strain of a ride on it! Bixby had thought about that little problem, of course. Too bad he never got the chance to make that one last test! See you next story. . . .

49

And now, hold on, because I have a really big story for you. The saying for this one is, "Be careful of what you wish for, because you just might get it."

THE BIG STAND-UP

My name is Bart Thompson. I'm a television engineer. You may not believe the story I'm about to tell you. But it's true, every word of it. I know, because it happened to me.

It all began the night I'd decided to work late at the TV studio where I was employed. Just about 12:30 it was, the time when everybody gets a little bleary.

"Coming, Bart?" asked my friend Jack, putting on his coat.

"You go ahead, Jack," I replied. "I'm going to hang around. I wasn't pleased with camera one's picture tonight. Think I'll try and align it better."

The night's transmission time was over, and

everyone had gone home. Jack was the last to leave. When he was gone, I went out onto the sound stage and rolled camera one over to the control room window. I pointed it at my seat inside and focused it carefully.

"You made the mayor's wife look like she weighed three hundred pounds tonight, baby," I addressed the camera, squinting into its eyepiece. "She's fat, but not *that* fat. You need some adjusting."

Then I went into the control room. I sat down at the monitor panel and flipped on camera one's monitor screen. Then I cut the juice and dropped the transmitter hookup so the image wouldn't go out over the air. Pretty soon, my own sad puss appeared on the panel.

"Boy, you *do* need adjusting, baby," I muttered to the camera. "I look like I just got slammed on the head with a sledgehammer!"

It was true. I looked squished down, the top of my head flat, my chin halfway into my neck.

I went out to the camera and increased the vertical drive. Then I checked the linearity and returned to my seat.

"There," I said. "That ought to . . . look . . .

HUH? Hey, who's kiddin' around?"

The face on camera one's monitor was not my face at all this time. It was the face of a beautiful girl. She had long, curly black hair, juicy red lips, and a metal helmet with pointy things on it that stuck up at the sides.

"Hey! What's the big idea?" I exclaimed. "Somebody tryin' to be funny?"

I flicked on the control room mike and the P.A. system. My voice echoed loudly through the studio. "Look, whoever you are!" I shouted. "I'm tryin' to get some work done. Stop the comedy and cut in camera one— *huh?*" My ranting came to a screeching halt as the figure on the screen began talking in some kind of gibberish.

"*Shul-mro-duh!*" said the beauty.

I was losing my temper fast. First that gorgeous face, and now some jive double-talk. "Climb off it!" I said. "I didn't stay late for fun! Jack? You doin' this?"

"*Crus-fon-duh-mor-nyd-ala-vort,*" replied the woman calmly.

I couldn't figure it out. Camera one was on. I could tell by the glowing red light on the top. And it was pointed directly at me. Yet the monitor in the control room carried the picture of that luscious babe. I pinched myself. I figured I must be dreaming.

"Ouch!" I cried. Well, I wasn't dreaming.

"*Ouch?*" repeated the woman. "*Quad-nort-dor-von-cost-du-mala-bod?*"

No, I was wide awake. Something freakish was taking place. Unless somebody had deliberately rewired the monitor board, this thing was impossible! But I nearly tore the place apart when she started talking English.

"Who . . . are . . . you? I . . . am . . . Lara! View . . . graph . . . engineer . . . 7B2R. Third . . . shift . . . Interplanetary Communications Commission! Headquarters Station . . . Zunda . . . on Planet 4."

"*Huh?*" I blurted. "Wha? Aw, cut it out,

will ya? That's enough foolin' around!" Whatever Jack was doing, it was really getting to me.

But she just kept on talking. And she was dead serious.

"Operation . . . of . . . Interplanetary Communications . . . is . . . not . . . fooling around! You . . . are . . . jamming . . . my . . . wavelength! Identify yourself!"

"Wha . . . ? Why—I—Listen, cutie pie!" I spluttered. "This is TV engineer Bart Thompson . . . Station WZYR-TV . . . Planet Earth . . . salary $730.50 per . . . and I'll knock your boyfriend's head off when I get ahold of—"

"Planet . . . *what?*" she said.

"Earth!" I repeated. "Like, he's gonna be buried six feet under! Look here, Jack! That's enough!" I was just waiting for him to jump out from somewhere, laughing madly. After I cooled off, the first thing I'd ask him would be where he'd gotten that crazy helmet.

"Earth?" she said, looking concerned. "In what solar system is your planet located?"

"In the solar system with the nine planets—including the one with the gigantic *ring*—which is just what I'm gonna do to your neck!"

I said, addressing the invisible Jack.

"The gigantic ring! But that is impossible!" she said.

That brought me up short. "Huh? What's impossible?"

"Your solar system," she said, "is eighty light-years away! The one with the big ring—it is the sixth planet from the star?"

"That's right. And I'm on the third: Earth. Say! Is this a joke, or isn't it?" My head was beginning to spin.

"This is no joke, Bart Thompson . . . Station WZYR-TV . . . salary $730.50 per! We are eighty light-years apart!"

I could see all of her now. She was magnificent, every inch of her. She was wearing a kind of sheer thing made of some metallic material, and her hair cascaded down her back. If this was how they made aliens, *The War of the Worlds* was very wrong indeed.

"Eighty light-years apart!" I said. "But that's impossible! Do you see *me?*"

"Very clearly," she answered.

"But I'm not even transmitting! I'm on a closed circuit!"

"Obviously," she said, as if talking to a three-year-old, "it is an interstellar electronic warp."

"Say!" I interjected. "How come I can understand you? If you're from some other world, how come you speak English?"

"I don't speak your language. I speak my own. You heard it before. I have an automatic translator hooked up. It's a type of mechanical electric brain. It translates our respective languages for us."

Well, Lara was lovely. We chatted for half the night. She told me all about her planet, and I told her all about Earth.

Finally, I screwed up all my courage to say it. "You . . . you're very beautiful, Lara," I told her.

"And you—are quite handsome, Bart," she replied. I guess the idea of handsomeness they had on Planet 4 was a little different from our own—thank goodness.

"You mentioned something about space travel," I said, leaning close into the screen. "Your people have it?"

"Oh, yes," she smiled. "We travel all over our solar system."

"But . . . you . . . you couldn't come here, could you?" I said. I would have given anything to touch her at that moment.

"We . . . we could," she said haltingly. "But it would take a very long time. Ten, maybe fifteen, rotations of your planet about its star." She looked away sadly.

We kept talking all night, and toward morning, nutty as it sounds, I confessed my feelings to Lara. "I love you, Lara. I know it's crazy—and useless—but I do!"

"Oh, Bart!" she said. "I love you, too!"

"Would you come to Earth, honey?" I pleaded. "I would wait for you!"

"We will see, Bart," she said. "Now I must sign off. The next shift is coming!"

"But Lara!" I cried. "Suppose we cannot make contact again?" I was desperate.

"I will note every instrument setting. You do the same! We will try. Good-bye. . . ."

And then she was gone. I checked everything carefully, noting each adjustment of the equipment in the control room. Then I went home.

The next night, as 12:30 AM rolled around, I marched toward the control room.

"Stayin' late *again*, Bart?" Jack asked me.

"That's right," I said. I couldn't wait for him to leave.

As soon as everyone was gone, I set up the equipment exactly as it had been the previous night. Lara came in sharp and clear.

"Darling!" I said. "I was so worried—that—it wouldn't work again! I thought about you all day!"

"Oh, Bart! I thought about you too!" she said.

So there we were, with another night to

talk. That night I learned that Lara's society had a marriage-family setup like ours.

"If—if you came to Earth, Lara . . . I'd marry you!" I said with feeling.

"Would you, dearest?" she said. "We'll see."

We went on like that for a year. Every night I'd talk to Lara across the void of space. We fell desperately and passionately in love. I longed for her! And then, one night, Lara appeared on my screen looking more excited than I'd ever seen her.

"I have wonderful news, darling!" she announced. "One of our scientists has just perfected a new type of space drive! It would only take half a rotation to get to your planet now!"

"Could—you . . . ?" I began, hardly daring to ask the question.

"I could steal the experimental rocket ship!" she said. "If I got away, they'd never be able to stop me—and I'd come to you! But if I were caught, it would mean my life!"

"My life is empty without you, Lara!"

"Then I will do it," she said. "But we must plan everything carefully. Very carefully."

We started by my transmitting maps of

Earth to Lara. It was important that she know exactly where to land.

"You've got the hemisphere and continent," I told her, pointing things out on a map held up to the screen. "Now here's a more detailed map of the area. See—you'll land here, on these salt flats."

I'd chosen the most barren area I could think of. I wanted to keep this whole thing quiet. After two weeks of planning and preparation, we were ready.

"Just come down as near to the blinking light as possible," I said to her in our last conversation. "That'll be me."

"Good-bye, Bart!" she said, looking longingly at the screen. "See you in—six months, you call it?"

"Yes, baby!" I said. "Six months! And—please—be careful! I . . . I love you so!"

"I'll be careful," she said. "I've already bribed the guard. It will be easy. Till we meet . . ."

And she faded away.

I tried to make contact with Lara the night after, but she didn't come in. I knew she was on her way.

The next six months were sheer agony—the agony of waiting. Finally the time drew near. I had to make my preparations.

"Remember that Jeep with the searchlight mounted on it that we used when that movie star came to town, Jack?" I asked him casually one night.

"Yep," he said. "We got it from the army. They said we could have it anytime."

I borrowed it. I gave the army a tall story about another movie star and drove out to the salt flats. As the hour drew near, I started flashing the light into the star-studded sky.

"Here, Lara!" I said out loud, trying to send

a signal from my mind to hers. "Right here, honey!"

Suddenly the sky above me was filled with a roaring, and the searchlight caught a gleaming silver shape.

"It's Lara! It's her ship!" I cried.

Lara's rocket ship dropped tail-first toward the flats to the north of me. "Baby! Baby! Come to papa!" I crowed.

The ship came to rest about a mile away. I sped across the flats toward it, the searchlight trained on it.

"What a ship! What a gal to fly it all alone!" I was yelling. "Oh, baby, am I gonna kiss you!"

As I neared Lara's ship, a strange thing began to happen.

"Lara! It's me! Bart! I'm . . . I'm . . . *Good Lord!*"

It was Lara's ship. It seemed to be splitting in two, straight up and down, from stem to stern. And as the two halves of the gigantic ship parted wider, and I saw what was inside, I screamed . . . *"Lara! Oh . . . no!"*

Lara looked exactly as she'd appeared on

the TV screen. The only trouble was, she stood about two hundred feet tall. . . .

Heh, heh. How's that for a tall tale? We tried to enter it in a short story contest, but they wouldn't take it. Well, Bart knew things would start looking up when Lara showed up—he just didn't know exactly how. They're very happy now, though. Bart lives in Lara's ear, and they've made a cozy little home on the spaceship.

For my next fictional fling, I have chosen a very grave tale indeed. Yep! It's told by a grave! So cuddle up to that corpse over there, and I'll begin the drama of dread and death called—

THE CRAVING GRAVE

The wind blows sadly across the gnarled and bent trees around me. It whispers past the cold stone monuments that the others proudly hold upward toward the night sky. But above me there is no cold stone for the wind to sing over. I lie silent, feeling the emptiness within me . . . the yearning. The others sigh contentedly, shifting and cracking, embracing their rigid charges, each grave with its one eternal occupant. But I, I am lonely. I am waiting.

I have waited like this through the centuries, watching the others around me, each in turn, open wide and take in their wards, cradling them happily. Each time the sobbing friends and relatives, each time the pious words as the coffins were lowered. And now I wait in this

64

old cemetery, off in a forgotten corner—the last empty grave.

I have lain fallow through the freezes and the thaws. On Sundays, I have listened to the mourners and rememberers come and cry upon the others and place flowers upon their bosoms. And I yearn for the day when I, too, will reach forth and draw my own charge into my own damp embrace. Oh, I would take such good care of my corpse!

But wait—what is it that I hear? Voices in the wind . . . voices in the night . . . voices over *me!*

"Here it is, Willie."

"Let's get to it, Al. Not much time left till mornin'."

They are men's voices. Two men.

And what is it that I feel? Cold steel rending my crust, cracking open my earth-skin.

"Ugh. Hard as a rock."

"Here. Use the pick."

There is swearing and grunting.

"Why don't people die in the summertime, when the ground is soft?"

"I'll tell my congressman. They'll pass a law."

There is laughing.

There is a trembling down deep within me, a surge of excitement and anticipation. The wind dies . . . and the laughter dies.

"How old was she?"

"Sixty-three."

All these years of waiting. All these years of longing and yearning and crying. They're almost over. Those men upon my chest—they're gravediggers.

And now it is morning. I lie with my insides torn from me and heaped up at my side. I lie open, feeling the sunlight, the cold air. I hear the crunching steps that I have heard so often . . . the grunts of the pallbearers that have never delivered unto me until this day. And I smile . . .

I listen with a drunken joy to the ceremony, feeling the mourners' feet upon my breast. There are not many mourners. A nephew, his wife, and a lawyer. But I do not care. It is not the grieving ones I am interested in. It is the one for whom they grieve.

"Ashes to ashes, dust to dust." The familiar words are spoken.

The coffin is lowered. I reach upward for it, accepting it, feeling its smoothness, and sensing its contents. My death-ward . . . my corpse-charge . . . my own.

"Come, Roland," says the preacher.

"Yes . . . yes, sir," sobs the young man.

The mourners leave. The gravediggers step forward with their shovels. I hold the coffin close as they return my soil-innards to me. They stand, finally, upon my repaired body, tamping down my outer skin, stitching up the wound.

"All right, Mr. Ambitious. That's enough. C'mon."

"Take it easy, Willie."

The gravediggers trudge off. I am fulfilled. The emptiness within me is gone. The yearning is vanished. The body lies guarded inside me. I whisper to it . . . soothing it . . . comforting it in its final rest.

The days and weeks pass. But the body does not lie at rest. The body within me is not at peace. There is a stirring inside the coffin. A fluttering . . . a scratching.

The body tells me her story. Her name is Cynthia Meadows. She was, like me, lonely all her life. She'd remained unmarried—yearning for the things her married sister enjoyed.

Plain Cynthia had sat with her pretty young sister, smiling at the sister's new baby. "It's a lovely baby boy, Myra," Cynthia had said. "What's his name?"

"I'm going to call him Roland," Myra had said.

Cynthia had lived her life alone, as I had lived mine: waiting. She'd watched her nephew, Roland, grow from babyhood to boyhood. He was a strange child, given to dreadful tantrums and long silences. He never seemed to have many friends. But he was always nice to his aunt Cynthia, and she loved him very much. And the empty years had crawled by, as they had for me.

Over time, Cynthia had made wise investments of the inheritance she'd shared with her sister, and she'd grown wealthy, while her sister—her sister had not fared quite so well.

Myra and her husband had come to Cynthia's home one night. They sat on her sofa, looking miserable. "George's business failed," Myra had explained. "He's lost every cent we had!"

"I'm sorry, Myra. I'll try to help you," Cynthia had said. And she had helped. She had gone without luxuries so that George and Myra could have a nice home for their son. They bought a big house in a nice neighborhood, and Cynthia went there for dinner twice a year.

And she'd waited through the years, as I'd waited. Finally, one day, George, Myra's husband, appeared at Cynthia's screen door while she was baking cookies.

"It's Myra, Cynthia!" he'd cried. "She's desperately ill. Please . . . come quickly!"

Myra's illness was sudden and devastating. She died within the week.

Again George sat on Cynthia's sofa. This time he wept. "What about Roland, Cynthia?" he'd sobbed. "What will I do with him?"

"I'll . . . I'll look after him, George," she'd said. "If you want me to."

And so, the lonely years had ended for Cynthia, as my lonely years had ended. She'd taken Roland to her bosom, as I'd taken her to mine.

Roland had cried bitterly at first. "But I want my mommy!"

"Your mother has gone away, Roland," Cynthia would explain, tears filling her own eyes. "She's gone away for a long time."

Roland's arrival in Cynthia's house had

meant the end of the loneliness . . . just as *her* arrival had meant the end of loneliness for me. She'd call him in for dinner every night, just like the other mothers. And she was happy.

Cynthia had guarded Roland and comforted him, and he'd grown into manhood. But eventually there was a stirring within him . . . just as now, Cynthia stirs.

"I'm going away, Aunt Cynthia," he'd said one day. "I can't stay here any longer." He would not look at her.

"Roland! Don't leave me! Please," she'd begged.

The scratching, clawing body within me tells how Roland had left her, despite her pleading . . . left her that same day.

And then she'd discovered why Roland had left so suddenly. She saw it when she opened her bureau drawer. "The money!" she'd gasped. "I had three thousand dollars in this drawer. It's gone!"

Poor Cynthia. How sorry I feel for her. To yearn for so long . . . to finally get her desire, and then to lose it once more. She tells me how brokenhearted she was, of how she'd cried for months.

She tells me how she'd tried to forget him. She tells me how she kept carefully investing the modest income she had, and how her investments had made her first comfortable and finally wealthy, wealthier than she'd been before.

And then, six years later, there was a knock on her door.

"Yes, who is it?" she said, peering through her screen door into the night. "Who . . . *Roland!* You've come back!"

"Yes, Aunt Cynthia. And I've brought someone." At his side was a good-looking young woman.

Cynthia had been so glad to see Roland that she'd completely forgotten the crime he'd committed when he left.

Roland presented the young woman. "This is my wife, Enid, Aunt Cynthia."

"Roland's told me so much about you, Aunt Cynthia!" said Enid, smiling as she dropped her coat into Cynthia's arms. "I'm so delighted to meet you!"

They'd come to live with her. Roland begged Cynthia's forgiveness. "I was young and foolish, Aunt Cynthia. It was wrong of me to take the money. I'm sorry."

"There, there, Roland," Cynthia had said. "It happened a long time ago." And she'd hugged him to her.

What a pretty picture they were! Cynthia knitted by the fire, Enid and Roland stood arm in arm by the mantelpiece. Cynthia did the dishes, Enid and Roland walked arm in arm upstairs to their bedroom. Cynthia washed the kitchen floor, Enid and Roland strolled arm in arm out the door to the movies.

"You don't know how happy you've made an old, lonely woman," she'd told them, mending one of Roland's socks.

"We both love you, Aunt Cynthia," they'd said sweetly.

But then Cynthia tells me what Roland and Enid had planned, in the privacy of their own bedroom. And now I know why the body I embrace within my earth-bed is not at peace. Now I know why it scratches and stirs inside. Cynthia Meadows was murdered.

Her niece and nephew had convinced her to change her will, leaving all her money to them, and then pushed her brutally down a long flight of cellar steps. Then they'd called the doctor.

"We heard her scream and fall," an agitated Roland had explained to the doctor. "We came as fast as we could! When we got here, she . . ."

"What a horrible, horrible accident!" Enid had sobbed, burying her face in her hands.

"She's . . . she's dead," said the doctor, horrified. He had been a friend.

The body within me turns and pushes and scratches. I try to stop it, try to make my insides hard. But it is determined. Then, one night, months after I first embraced it, the body

pushes upward into the cool air, pushing out-
ward past my crust-skin. A hand claws at the
moonlight.

Despite my pleading, the body totters off,
across the other graves, into the cold wind.

We were the same, Cynthia and I . . . lonely
and waiting. And then the waiting had ended
for both of us. Roland was given to her, and
she to me. But just as Roland left Cynthia to
the loneliness and misery, she too has left me.
Now I can only do as she did: try to forget.

The wind blows sadly across the gnarled and bent trees that surround me. It whispers past the cold stones. I lie silent with the emptiness within me, and I wait.

And then, one night, far away, I hear it: the screaming.

Something is coming toward me, dragging the screaming behind it.

It is Cynthia. She drags them along, holding them in her vise-like grip, and staggers across the other graves toward me. She holds them, Roland and Enid—holds them out to me. They are still screaming.

And I reach for them. Cynthia helps me reach. She shoves aside my skin-crust, scoops out my insides, pushes them, shrieking, into my embrace. . . .

Cynthia is gone away now. The screaming has stopped. Yes, we were alike, she and I. Each waited. Each got what she waited for, only to lose it again. But what we lost was eventually returned to us. Roland's and Enid's twisted and suffocated bodies lie deep within me, pressed against my earth-bosom. And now it is I who can laugh, laugh at the others.

For I now know real fulfillment. I'm not like the others. I'm special! After all, the others are all single graves, with just one body each. And I—I have two!

Heh, heh. And so, kiddies, our sorry story ends on this grave note. Roland and Enid were punished for their crime, buried alive by Cynthia's corpse, and our little grave rotted them happily ever after. And where's Cynthia these days, you ask? Why, she wandered around till she found some other lonesome grave and just . . . dropped in. Isn't that nice?

For our next story, we come back down to earth with a plop. In this one, we learn the real, true meaning of the phrase "hungry for love."

RAW DEAL

Often, during the long, dark night, the halls of the psychiatric ward would echo with his scream. It was a scream of terror, from a poor lost soul wandering in mental purgatory. His ear-splitting yell would frighten the other patients behind their doors, and startle even the night nurses out of their cold, trained calm. This shriek in the night was always the same . . . the same three words . . . shattering the hospital silence with their quivering reverberations.

"I hate her! I hate her! I hate her!"

The head nurse of the psychiatric ward covered her ears. "There he goes again, Agnes!" she wailed. "You take him this time, huh? Room 212. Gregg Bolton . . . Lord, if he keeps

78

this up, I'll go out of my mind!"

"That screaming is enough to rattle anyone, Sally," said the other night nurse. "Give me the hypodermic. I'll quiet him down."

There was no use trying to soothe the tortured screamer. The nurses had learned that long ago. Only a hypodermic needle filled with the correct amount of a powerful sedative could send him back into a drugged, moaning, tossing sleep.

"There," sighed Agnes after giving the shot. "He's out."

"He's been like that ever since they brought him in. For three weeks . . . screaming . . . yelling those same three words. Will Dr. Swanson ever start curing him?" Sally wondered aloud.

Gregg Bolton was one of Allen Swanson's most difficult psychiatric patients. The doctor had tried every means at his disposal to end the poor man's continuous raving, including electroshock therapy.

Late that night he sat over the patient, fussing with the dials on the electroshock machine. "This is his fifth shock," he said to himself. "If he doesn't come out of it now . . ." The doctor shook his head.

But the fifth shock didn't help. Nothing helped. The nightly screaming continued, and all of the doctor's efforts to make Gregg talk, to unburden his tortured mind, led only to the same three words.

"*I hate her!*" shrieked Bolton, tossing frantically in his bed.

"Gregg," said Dr. Swanson intensely, leaning close over him, "Gregg, you must try to listen to me . . . try to *answer* me. *Who* do you hate? *Who?*"

Finally, in desperation, Dr. Swanson called in an eminent consultant: the world-renowned Dr. John Peabody.

"I need your advice, John," he said. "It's this Bolton case. I can't seem to break through to him. He's getting progressively worse."

"Hmmm," said Peabody, looking over the patient's chart. "I see you've given him the works. What's his clinical history, Allen?"

"He's the sole survivor of a plane crash in the Pacific," said Swanson. "A luxury airliner bound for Hawaii. Halfway there, the plane went down in flames and sank. Out of forty-five passengers, he alone was found—after five weeks. He was floating at sea in a small rubber raft."

"Poor chap." The specialist glanced over at the wildly staring patient. "That would be enough to unhinge any mind."

"There's more, John," said Swanson. "One of the registered passengers was his bride! They were on their honeymoon. They'd been married less than six hours when the plane went down . . . six short hours!"

"Sad," commented Peabody. "He obviously suffered a severe mental trauma brought about by intense grief plus the strain of the experience itself . . . drifting alone for five weeks . . . thinking of his lost happiness . . . his love snatched

81

from him. Symptoms, of course, are deep depression, suicidal tendencies—hysteria?"

"Yes," said Swanson. "Plus one odd factor, John. One thing I can't fit in. In his nightmares and in our talks, he consistently shouts the same three words: 'I hate her!' Whom could he be talking about?"

"Hmmm. Certainly not his bride. Perhaps someone else on the plane? Perhaps . . . Allen, we've got to pin it down! We've got to break through so we can perform a decent interrogation and perhaps cure him! I suggest we use pentothal."

And so, the maximum dosage of sodium pentothal was injected into the patient. The popularly known "truth drug" had the power to overcome deep barriers within the sick mind, allowing its troubles to pour out. But only three words erupted from Gregg Bolton's lips: *"I hate her! I hate her!"*

"*Who*, Gregg?" demanded Peabody. "Tell us who you hate! Tell us everything!"

At last, after hours of this, the truth serum worked its wonders, dredging Gregg Bolton up from the bottomless pit into which he had plunged.

"Gregg! Answer me! You hate *whom?*" Peabody was saying for the fiftieth time.

Suddenly the patient seemed to be waking from a long, bad dream. "I hate . . . I hate . . . *eh?* Why . . . uh . . . Linda! I . . . I hate Linda!"

Dr. Swanson looked at Dr. Peabody. "*Linda?* His *bride?* How could he hate the girl he'd just married? It doesn't make sense, John! It doesn't even make the right kind of nonsense for a psychiatrist . . . unless it's inverted wording, disguised true feeling."

"Wait, Allen," advised Peabody. "Let's not jump to conclusions here." The older psychiatrist spoke slowly, with the distilled wisdom of long experience in dealing with troubled human minds. "Sometimes we tangle ourselves in complexities when simplicities are the right answer. That trite saying—love is close to hate—might fit Gregg. Keep him talking. Give him another five cc's."

"As you wish, John," said Swanson. He measured another dose of pentothal into the hypodermic needle.

"Tell us, Gregg!" Peabody said, bending over the poor, deranged man. "Tell us why you hate Linda!"

"Tell us the whole story," urged Swanson.

The second dose took dramatic effect. Gregg began talking, slurring his words a bit. But once he started talking, he just kept going.

"Linda!" he said. "I . . . I met her three months ago at a party. Sweet, lovely Linda." He stared straight ahead of him, at the wall.

"Beautiful, gracious Linda," he continued. "We were introduced . . . we danced . . . we fell in love. It was lightning-fast. Neither of us had any doubt, from the very first moment.

"'Linda,' I said to her as we sat under a tree, the lights and the noise of the party in the distance, 'I've known you all my life . . . longer!'

"'Yes, Gregg!' she said. 'We met a billion years ago!'

"Our first burning kiss sealed our love forever. It was a tender love, passionate, divine. We loved until we ached with an infinite joy that nearly burst our hearts.

"Funny how convention rules us. Only my sense of propriety made me wait a decent interval—a month—before whispering the age-old words that rang for us with a magic wonder and newness.

"'Marry me, Linda?' I asked her. 'Be my wife?'

"'Oh, yes, Gregg!' she replied. 'Yes, yes, yes!'"

Gregg Bolton stirred in the bed. "No love more sublime ever existed in this crazy world of ours," he said. "She was everything to me! More than life! How could I tell you? Linda was . . . she was . . . uh . . . she. . ."

But then, as the effect of the pentothal wore off, Gregg's face suddenly contorted. His body writhed. His fists clenched. And from loving tenderness, his voice changed to a harsh shriek.

"Linda? I hate her! *I hate her!*"

Dr. Peabody furrowed his brow. "Puzzling,"

he said. "Very puzzling."

The two psychiatrists struggled with their screaming patient, forcing him back down upon the pillow.

"That's all the pentothal we can risk giving him today, John," said Allen. "I'll hold him. You'd better give him a sedative."

"Strange," mused the other doctor, administering the shot. "His complete reversal of feelings . . ."

They stood in the hall outside the patient's room, listening to his cries fade.

"*I hate her* . . . I hate her . . . hate . . . her. . . ."

"Well, John?" said Allen. "Is this one a corker or isn't it? One minute telling us of his heavenly love for Linda, the next moment screaming *that!*"

"Something must have happened later on in his story, Allen," said Peabody. "I'll be back tomorrow. We'll give him another pentothal shot then."

And they went home to ruminate about the strange case of Gregg Bolton.

Early the next morning, the truth drug launched Gregg further into his story. The two psychiatrists listened closely.

"We were married soon after," said Gregg, lying quietly now in his bed. "And Linda was mine—all mine. After the wedding party, we had no time to be alone. Our plane—our honeymoon plane—was waiting to take us to Hawaii. We rushed directly to the airport.

" 'Only a few more hours, darling,' I said to her, 'and then we'll be there. Hawaii . . . the Royal Palms Hotel . . . alone at last!'

" 'The honeymoon suite! Oh, darling— alone!' Linda nestled into my shoulder. I was so happy.

"Neither of us realized how those words she had said would come true in a different and horrifying way, for then . . . oh, God . . . I'll never forget. One engine started to cough and sputter. The stewardess tried to reassure us. 'Please be calm, ladies and gentlemen,' she said. 'We're having trouble with the outside right engine. The pilot will feather the propeller. We still have three engines—more than enough to remain aloft.'

"Linda clutched my arm. 'Oh, Gregg, I'm afraid!' she cried.

" 'Don't worry, hon,' I started to say. 'It—'

"But then, suddenly, the lurid red glare erupting from the conked-out engine ... the dying motor giving up the ghost in licking flame ... !

"'Fire! We're on fire!' somebody shouted.

"'Oh, Lord!' I heard myself say.

"We plummeted seaward, like a meteor, leaving a smoking, screaming trail.

"The plane was a funeral pyre, floating and burning, cremating its passengers for their watery grave. Screams ... dying shrieks and moans ... the greedy gurgle and hiss of the mountainous waves ... it was all a hellish confused madness!"

The patient moved his arms and legs in agitation but continued his story.

"Don't ask me how Linda and I escaped. All I remember is that somehow we got out through the emergency exit door beside our seats before the plane went down, and there was an emergency life raft inflating itself from an attached bottle of compressed gas.

"I don't even remember climbing aboard the raft or pulling Linda in after me. When we came out of our dazed shock, we realized the terrible truth.

" 'N-Nobody else is swimming away,' I said.

" 'No more screams!' said Linda. 'Just . . . silence!' She began to sob.

"And then our happy words came back to haunt us with their horrible meaning. 'Gregg!' Linda gasped. 'We're alone! All alone!'

" 'Alone in the Pacific!' I said."

As Gregg paused in his narrative, with the bitterness of that moment etched in his pain-lined face, the two psychiatrists exchanged significant glances.

"So," whispered Swanson to Peabody, "Linda *survived* the plane crash with him! An unexpected turn! We had assumed, since he was picked up alone in the raft, that he was the sole survivor. But . . . then . . . what happened to her? *What happened to Linda?*"

"Hush," whispered Peabody. "He's going on."

Gregg's voice was a bit weaker now, but he continued to remember the dreadful things that had befallen him. "Forty-three people . . . burned . . . drowned," he intoned. "We put the tragedy out of our minds. There was nothing we could do for them. All that mattered, really, was that we were alive—and we had to *stay* alive.

"After a little while, it began to rain. It was cold, but it was beautiful to us. 'Drink!' I told her. 'Drink all you can! There's no telling how long we'll drift before we're rescued!'

"We were alive, yes. But what torture . . . what refined, exquisite torture. That tiny rubber raft . . . our 'nuptial suite,' our 'honeymoon idyll'!

"I held her shaking body in my arms. 'Oh, Linda, Linda, my poor darling,' I said, 'cold, wet, shivering, miserable . . . here, instead of in a cozy hotel warmed by our love.' She just sobbed and sobbed.

"Misery swiftly became utter wretchedness as the rains turned into violent storms that nearly pitched us into the sea. But far worse was the fog and the calm that followed—the deadly, monotonous, mind-smothering horror of just floating in the gray mist, listening help-lessly as an occasional search plane droned by high overhead.

"And after the fog, when the search planes had given up and no longer combed the area, the sun began to beat down unmercifully. Thirst was a parching fire in our throats. Hunger joined forces with thirst, gnawing at our in-sides. We had snatched not even a crumb from the wreck.

"'Gregg! Gregg . . . I'm starving!' Linda moaned. And I could only look up to heaven and beg for help.

"We'd just about given up when a flying fish blundered aboard our raft, and we pounced upon it with animal growls. 'Rip it apart, Linda!' I yelled. 'Don't waste a drop! Not even the guts!'

"She gnawed on that fish, holding it with her bare hands. It was raw, but to her it was delicious.

"But after the fish, nothing. Not a bite, except for the few handfuls of seaweed I managed to scoop up with my hands. Maggots ate at my soul as I watched my beloved grow thinner and thinner, wasting away. Her voice was barely audible. 'So . . . hungry,' she whispered feebly. 'And no ship . . . no plane. It's hopeless . . . hopeless . . . .'

"I did all I could to keep her alive. Finally, I had the idea of taking off my belt. 'Here, chew it,' I said to her. 'It will help kill that emptiness inside.'

" 'Oh, Gregg,' she whispered. 'Our love . . . at least nothing will kill that!'

"The fever . . . the thirst . . . the hunger-rats gnawing away in our guts . . . the eternities of straining to see a ship on the horizon, a plane in the vast blue above . . . they could not stop us from holding each other, warming ourselves with our love each cold, bitter night.

"Yes, if that frightful ordeal proved nothing else, it proved that our love was unshakable, steadfast, utterly impervious to anything! To the last, Linda loved me—and I loved Linda!"

Bolton stared hollow-eyed at the ceiling, a haunted man.

"Gregg!" said Dr. Swanson. "When you were picked up, you were alone! What happened to Linda?"

"What happened to Linda?" Gregg repeated bitterly. "Can't you guess, Doctor? Day after endless day . . . sitting there . . . opposite me . . . under the broiling sun . . . starving . . . starving! She started to babble . . . to rave . . . to go out of her mind. She saw things that weren't there . . . heard things . . .

" 'Hear it, Gregg?' she said, insanely cheerful. 'It's a plane! There it is! There! Wave to it, Gregg! Make them see us!'

" 'There isn't any plane, Linda!' I hollered,

holding her by the shoulders. 'Stop it! *Stop it!*'

"Thirst must have made her drink seawater when I wasn't looking. Before my eyes, in those last days, I watched my love writhe . . . and scream in agony . . . and gag . . . and retch . . . and cough up bile . . . and finally, mercifully, die! I sobbed over her limp body. 'Linda!' I cried. 'Come back!' But of course, she wasn't coming back at all."

There was a hushed moment. A tear stole down Gregg's gaunt, ravaged face. There was a warm look in his eyes, a faraway look. His lips twisted into a half-smile. Dr. Swanson bent forward, impatient for him to go on.

"But then . . . when did you begin to hate her, Gregg?" he asked, his face close to the patient's. "What *happened?* Go on!"

But Dr. Peabody intervened, interrupting Swanson. "Leave him alone, Allen!" he ordered.

Swanson shook Gregg. Gregg's eyes darkened. His face grew taut, ashen. He shuddered. He screamed: "*I hate her!*"

"Blast it!" Swanson cursed. "He's gone off again! I'll give him another five cc's."

"Don't bother, Allen," said Peabody.

Dr. Swanson stood up. He turned to Dr. Peabody.

"*I hate her! I hate her!*" Gregg was screaming hoarsly.

"Listen to him!" Swanson shouted at Peabody in frustration. "We'll never know what happened if I don't give him—"

Peabody cut him short. "There's no need for another shot," he said quietly. "I know what happened."

"You *know?* You know why he changed—why his love changed to hate?"

"His love never changed," said Peabody. He began to pace the room. "The mind is a strange thing, Allen . . . yours . . . mine. Memory association sometimes tricks us. We hear what we want to hear. Sometimes we hear wrong."

"Hear wrong, John?"

"The man was alive after five weeks in a life raft, Allen. How could a man stay alive with no provisions—no water—for five weeks?"

"*I hate her!*" shrieked the patient, writhing on the bed.

"He's not saying *hate,* Allen," said Peabody. "Listen closely. He's telling you what he did after Linda died. He's telling us exactly how he

95

stayed alive!"

Swanson buried his head in his hands. "Good Lord!" he rasped in a shaky voice.

"*I hate her!*" Gregg Bolton was yelling, staring wildly up at the ceiling.

. . . and so, my little rug rats, there's a lesson to be learned here: Listen very carefully to those around you, because they might not be saying what you think they're saying. For instance, if your best friend says, "My mother says we can have you for dinner," maybe you'd better think twice about going. . . .